Sandy Creek
NEW YORK

An Imprint of Sterling Publishing
387 Park Avenue South
New York, NY 10016

That's When I'm Happy: Text © Beth Shoshan, Illustration © Jacqueline East. First published 2005 by Meadowside Children's Books.
If You Can...We Can: Text © Beth Shoshan, Illustration © Petra Brown. First published 2008 by Meadowside Children's Books.
Little Rabbit Waits for the Moon: Text © Beth Shoshan, Illustration © Stephanie Peel. First Published 2004 by Meadowside Children's Books.
Cuddle!: Text © Beth Shoshan, Illustrations © Jacqueline East. First Published 2006 by Meadowside Children's Books.
Wide Awake Jake: Text © Rachel Elliot, Illustration © Karen Sapp. First published 2004 by Meadowside Children's Books.
If Big Can...I Can: Text © Beth Shoshan, Illustration © Petra Brown. First published 2006 by Meadowside Children's Books.
My Favorite Food: Text © Tiziana Bendall-Brunello, Illustration © John Bendall-Brunello.
First published 2010 by Gullane Children's Books.

This 2013 edition published by Sandy Creek.

ISBN 978-1-4351-4733-1

Manufactured in Heshan, China
Lot #:
2 4 6 8 10 9 7 5 3 1
04/13

Goodnight
Stories Collection

Sandy Creek
NEW YORK

Contents

Cuddle!

I'd cuddle a whale,
but I might be too small,

9

I'd cuddle
a hedgehog
but, **ouch!**
they're so spiky,

11

I'd cuddle a crocodile.

Hmmm...?

Not likely!

13

If I cuddled
a gorilla

I would end up
much thinner,

If I cuddled a tiger
I'd end up as dinner.

17

I'd cuddle a skunk
but I think they're
too smelly,

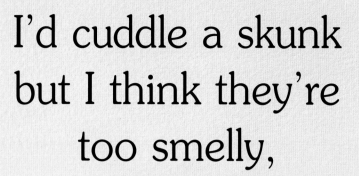

18

I'd cuddle a shark

but I'd be in his belly!

21

I'd cuddle
a python

way up high
in a tree,

I'd cuddle a hippo
who might just
squash me.

24

I'd cuddle a lion

but he'd bite off my head,

25

Do you think
I can cuddle
**my teddy bear
instead?**

Little *Rabbit* *Waits for the* Moon

Little Rabbit
couldn't sleep...

In the day,
the sun is there, warm
and bright. But when night comes,
the sky hangs low, dark, and empty.

30

"If I fall asleep now, there'll be no one
watching over me," thought Little Rabbit.
"I'll just have to wait for the moon."
And so he did just that.

The trouble with being so tired and sleepy, was that he didn't know exactly when the moon would come.

More time passed and the moon still hadn't come.

"This is my first day, ever,"
said a small flower in the fields.
"Maybe I will have grown into a tree
by the time your moon comes."

That sounded like a very long time.

Little Rabbit thought he had better ask
someone else—just to be sure.

35

"Look deep into the water," shimmered a little lake nearby. "Maybe your moon has fallen in and can't get out."

That didn't sound like what he wanted to hear.

Little Rabbit thought he had better ask someone else—just to be sure.

"Why don't you walk with me?"
twisted a long and winding path.
"We can find out where I'm leading
and maybe your moon is at the
other end!"

That sounded like it might
be a long way away.

Little Rabbit thought he had better ask
someone else—just to be sure.

"I've just blown in to these parts," breezed a wind that had picked up. "Who knows? I might be a big, fierce storm by the time your moon comes."

That didn't sound like something he wanted to wait for.

Little Rabbit thought he had better ask someone else—just to be sure.

42

"We can't see your moon yet,"
rumbled the great, rolling hills.
"And we can see far into
the distance from up here!"

That didn't sound very promising.

Little Rabbit began to think that the
moon might never come. And he was
getting very, very tired…

And then, from behind the hills,
carried by the wind along the twists
of the path, reflected in the lake, and shining
on the petals of the small flower…

44

...the most perfect moon
slid into the night sky.

45

But Little Rabbit
had fallen asleep, dreaming
of the moon that would
watch over him through the night.

If Big can...
I can...

If Big can run...
...then I can run

(Though not as fast,
I'm only small)

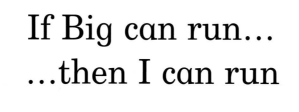

If Big can jump...
...then I can jump

(And Big leaps long,
long, long away)

If Big can swing…
…then I can swing

(As Big swings
high into the sky,
I'll get there too,
one day, I'm sure)

If Big can climb…
…then I can climb

(It's just I have to take my time to get to all the places Big can climb to with one stretch)

If Big can see...
...then I can saw

56

(Up, up I go, into the air.
I never thought I'd get so high,
but now that Big is on the ground
how will I get down?)

If Big can play...

58

...then I can play

(Deep in the sand Big digs a hole...

...but if I fell in I'd be stuck and then I'd have to
yell and shout for Big to come and pull me out)

59

But what if Big
can't get in places
only I can squeeze inside?

I'd find the treasures,

Rule the roost!

Be number one...

And Big would know
I'm having fun.

If Big could only see...

...how great it is
inside my den and all
the games I like to play
on oceans around the world
and spaceships in the sky.

Here I can swing into the air!

Running fast and leaping long

66

and stretch to climb
and soaring high
into the air
and digging deep…

…but Big's not there…

67

...I'm all alone...

...and that's no fun,

so...

Whatever Big can...

and whatever I can...

That's When I'm Happy!

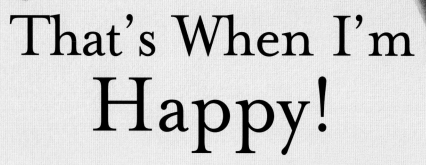

There are some days
when I'm very happy...
and there are some days
when I'm a little bit sad.

But now, on those days
when I'm a little bit sad...
I try and find my way back
to being happy.

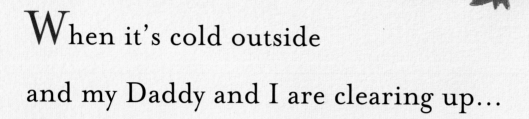

When it's cold outside
and my Daddy and I are clearing up...

And when we take a soft striped bag
and fill it up with leaves...

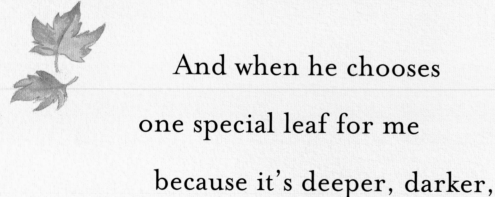

And when he chooses

one special leaf for me

because it's deeper, darker,

redder than all the others...

And when my Daddy

and I play soccer

through the leaves

and we're kicking

to each other

through a tunnel of trees...

...that's when I'm happy!

When it's cozy inside and my
Mommy and I give each other
great big bear hugs...

And when we rub our noses together...

And when she chooses one
special tickle, just for me
because it's wiggly,
squirmy, and makes me laugh
more than all the others...

And then my Mommy
gives me the biggest kiss of all...

And I reach up to give her a big kiss back...

But not as big,
because my mouth is still very small...

...that's when I'm happy!

When it's night outside

and my Daddy and I gaze through the window...

And when he takes my hand

and points at the night sky...

And when he chooses one special star

for me because it's bigger,

burning brighter than all the others...

84

85

And then my Daddy
and I count all the stars
in the sky, and he says
there are more than 119...

But I can't count any higher...

...that's when I'm happy!

When it's warm inside and my Mommy

and I run our fingers through the books...

And when we look at all the pictures...

And when she chooses

one special book for me

because it's our favorite,

better than all the others...

88

89

And then my Mommy reads
the perfect story to me
and I can read some
of the words...

But mostly the ones
with the letters
from my name in them...

...that's when I'm happy!

When it's dark everywhere

and I cuddle up

to my Mommy and Daddy

(even though they're asleep)

still telling stories to myself,

watching stars in the sky,

bathed in all their kisses,

and dreaming of the deep

red leaves...

92

That's when we're happy!

If You Can...
We Can!

I love you…

I really do!

(Although my arms are just too small
and so I can't quite cuddle you.)

I hug you...
you hug me.

(And around
and around
we dance together,
holding tight.

Don't let me fall!)

I tickle you...
you giggle too.

(But not my toes...! No!
Not my toes,
you know that's when I'll squeal the most!)

I make you laugh...
you laugh with me.

(There's nothing in this world
that can make us feel so good
as laughter can, as laughter does,
as laughter should.)

I hold your hand...
you hold mine tight.

(Just feeling snug, secure, and safe.
Just knowing you'll protect me,
care for me...
be there.)

I sing you songs...
   you sing them too.

(Loud ones, soft ones,
   make-me-laugh ones.
Love songs, sleep songs,
   safe-and-sound songs.)

I tell you tales…
you listen close.

(Then tell me stories
through the night...

of mighty dragons,
gallant knights...

adventures made
to fill my mind.)

109

I'm in your dreams...
and you're
in mine.

(The best dreams, safe dreams,
sleep-all-night dreams.
My dreams, your dreams.
Always our dreams.)

Let's be friends forever, I say!

There for one another,
looking out and taking care.

So...

112

Whatever you do...

114

and whatever I do…

Let's do it...

...together!

Wide
Awake Jake

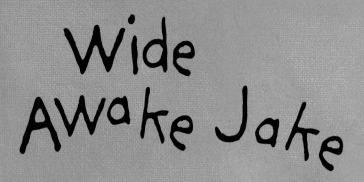

Jake couldn't sleep.

He lay on his back.

He lay on his tummy.

He even lay upside down.

But it was **no** good.

He was **still** wide awake.

So Jake got up and went downstairs...

HUFF
PUFF
HUFFITY
PUFF

120

"I can't sleep," huffed Jake.

"Try counting sheep," said Dad.

But Jake didn't think **that** would help.

"Pretend you're a little bear,
going to sleep for the winter,"
said Mom.

Jake thought that **could** work.

So he went back upstairs...

pad

pad

pad

Jake curled up inside his blanket.

"I'm a little bear,

grrr, grrr,"

he growled.

But then he heard noises.

What if it was a great BIG bear?
It might have long, sharp claws
and huge, yellow teeth!

And his fur was very itchy.

Jake, the little bear,
was still wide awake.
So he got up

and went downstairs...

125

THUMP

BUMP

CLUMPITY

THUMP

"I can't sleep," grumbled Jake.

"Count to a million," said Dad.

Jake didn't think **that** would help.

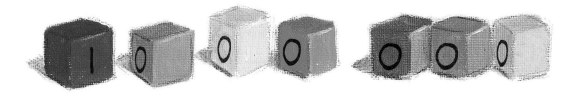

"Pretend you're a little mouse,
going to sleep in a mousehole,"
said Mom.

Jake thought that **could** work.

So he went back upstairs...

squeak

squeak

squeak

Jake crawled to the bottom of his bed.
But then he heard noises.
It might be a
big
fat
cat!!!
"Eek!" squeaked Jake,
the little mouse.
HURRY
FLURRY
SCURRY

"I can't sleep," worried Jake.

Dad just sighed.

Jake didn't think **that** was very helpful.

"Pretend you're a baby bird
in your nest,"
said Mom.

Jake thought it was worth a try.

So he went back upstairs...

flutter

flutter

flutter

Jake pulled his pillow under the covers.

"I'm a baby bird,
sitting in my nest,"
he whispered.
But his feathers kept

making him sneeze.

Then he
heard
noises!

Somebody was
pulling the
covers
down...

134

It was a big, hairy bear!

No, it didn't have any claws.

It was a fat, scary cat!

No, it didn't have a tail.

It was a big, scowly owl!

No, it didn't have a beak.

It was Mom!

Mom put the pillows straight.
She tucked Jake in,
nice and **tight**.

"You're my **brave** little Jake,
safe in your very own bed,"
said Mom.

"Now close your eyes.
It's time to sleep."

And with a **growly** yawn,

and a **mouse-quiet** wink,

and a **fluttery blink,**

Jake, the little boy,
was fast asleep.

My Favorite Food

Little Goose and her mommy were in the yard, enjoying some fresh, green grass.

140

"Mmm . . . I love grass,"
said Little Goose. "It's
my favorite food!

I wonder if everybody
loves grass as much as me?"

"Why don't you go and
find out," said Mommy.

So off went Little Goose to
find out Pig's favorite food . . .

141

"What's your favorite food, Pig?"
she asked.

"Apples,"

said Pig. "They're so juicy!"

142

143

"Mmm," said Little Goose, "I like apples too.
I wonder what Goat's favorite food is?"

So off she went to find out . . .

145

"What's your favorite food, Goat?"
asked Little Goose.

"Socks,"
said Goat. "They're so chewy!"

146

147

"Hmmm," said Little Goose,
"I'm not sure I like socks!

I wonder what Cow's favorite food is?"

148

So off she went to find out . . .

"What's your favorite food, Cow?" asked Little Goose.

"Daisies,"
said Cow. "They're so sweet!"

151

"Mmm," said Little Goose, "daisies are tasty.
But I wonder what Fox's
favorite food is?"

So off she went to find out . . .

"Fox! Fox! What's your favorite food?" asked Little Goose.

"Well . . ." said Fox,
"let me think.
My favorite food is . . ."

155

156

"YOU!"

"Yikes!" squealed Little Goose.
And she ran away as fast as her
little legs would carry her . . .

157

. . . safely back into
the loving wings
of her mommy.

And while Little Goose enjoyed some of her
favorite food—grass—

Fox settled down to eat his favorite food—strawberries!

160